HAVE YOU EVER WONDERED WHAT IT WOULD BE LIKE TO BATTLE . . .

SERPERIOR VS. SWANNA?

EMBOAR AND EMOLGA?

SAMUROTT AGAINST SIMISEAR?

Now's your chance! In this book, it's up to YOU to match up your favorite Unova Pokémon. Flip the pages to line up the Pokémon, head-to-head.

How do you decide who wins? Well, start by learning a bit more about your Pokémon's type. . . .

POKÉMON TYPES

Every Pokémon has a type — like Grass, Water, or Fire. Type tells you a lot about a Pokémon, particularly what moves it's likely to use in battle and how well it will do in battle against another type.

THERE ARE SEVENTEEN DIFFERENT POKÉMON TYPES:

We'll help you figure out who will win each battle by telling you what types each Pokémon's types are powerful against, and what kinds of moves the Pokémon is weak against. We'll also give you some inside info on your Pokémon's stats and battle strengths.

Ready to get in on the action? Let's begin!

STATS:

Type: Fire-Fighting
Height: 5' 03"
Weight: 330.7 lbs.

BATTLE STRENGTH: Emboar's beard puts foes in a hairy situation! It sets its fists ablaze by brushing them against its fiery chin. It can learn moves like Rollout and Head Smash to counter Flying-type opponents.

POWERFUL AGAINST: Bug, Dark, Grass, Ice, Normal, Rock, and Steel

WEAK AGAINST: Flying, Ground, Psychic, and Water

MEGA FIRE PIG POKÉMON

EMBOAR

STATS:

Type: Normal
Height: 3' 07"
Weight: 59.5 lbs.

BATTLE STRENGTH: Watchog is always on the lookout for enemies. When it encounters one, its tail points up and the markings on its body glow. It uses moves like Leer and Mean Look against foes.

POWERFUL AGAINST: Normal-types are not strong against any particular type, but Ghost-type attacks cannot damage them.

WEAK AGAINST: Fighting

LOOKOUT POKÉMON

WATCHOG

Type: Dark
Height: 3' 07"
Weight: 82.7 lbs.

BATTLE STRENGTH: Liepard likes to make surprise entrances and exits. Its favorite trick? Sneaking up on foes and attacking from behind their backs! It is known for sly moves like Torment, Taunt, and Nasty Plot.

POWERFUL AGAINST: Ghost and Psychic

WEAK AGAINST: Bug and Fighting

CRUEL POKÉMON

LIEPARD

STATS:

Type: Fire
Height: 3' 03"
Weight: 61.7 lbs.

BATTLE STRENGTH: Simisear loves sugar, which fuels the flame burning inside its body. When it's all fired up, Simisear can shoot embers from its head and the tip of its tail.

POWERFUL AGAINST: Grass, Ice, Bug, and Steel

WEAK AGAINST: Ground, Rock, and Water

EMBER POKÉMON

SIMISEAR

STATS:

Type: Normal-Flying
Height: 3' 11"
Weight: 63.9 lbs.

BATTLE STRENGTH: A wave of the long feathers on a male Unfezant's head is enough to strike fear in the hearts of many Pokémon. This Pokémon is strong and fast, and it can recharge itself in battle if it learns the self-healing move Roost.

POWERFUL AGAINST: Bug, Fighting, and Grass

WEAK AGAINST: Electric, Ice, and Rock

PROUD POKÉMON

UNFEZANT

STATS:

Type: Rock
Height: 5' 07"
Weight: 573.2 lbs.

BATTLE STRENGTH: The orange crystals on Gigalith's body soak up energy from the sun. When Gigalith is charged up, its mouth shoots energy blasts that can turn towering mountains into piles of rubble. Its Ability, Sturdy, can keep it standing after even the most powerful attacks.

POWERFUL AGAINST: Bug, Flying, Fire, and Ice

WEAK AGAINST: Fighting, Grass, Ground, Steel, and Water

COMPRESSED POKÉMON

GIGALITH

Type: Ground-Steel
Height: 2' 04"
Weight: 89.1 lbs.

BATTLE STRENGTH: With its superstrong steel drill, Excadrill can bore a hole in a metal plate — which is bad news even for Pokémon with strong armor! Ice- and Rock-types should beware its Metal Claw attack.

POWERFUL AGAINST: Electric, Fire, Ice, Poison, Rock, and Steel

WEAK AGAINST: Fighting, Fire, Ground, and Water

SUBTERRENE POKÉMON

EXCADRILL

STATS:

Type: Water-Ground
Height: 4' 11"
Weight: 136.7 lbs.

BATTLE STRENGTH: When Seismitoad makes the knobs on its fists pulse, it can turn a rock into rubble with one swing. The humps on its head shoot a liquid that paralyzes foes. Its combination of types makes it a powerful adversary.

POWERFUL AGAINST: Electric, Fire, Ground, Poison, Rock, and Steel

WEAK AGAINST: Grass

VIBRATION POKÉMON

SEISMITOAD

STATS:

Type: Fighting
Height: 4' 02"
Weight: 112.4 lbs.

BATTLE STRENGTH: Like Throh, Sawk's belt plays a powerful part in battle. When it pulls its belt, Sawk's punch becomes more aggressive — and so does its attitude.

POWERFUL AGAINST: Dark, Ice, Normal, Rock, and Steel

WEAK AGAINST: Flying and Psychic

KARATE POKÉMON

SAWK

STATS:

Type: Bug-Poison
Height: 8' 02"
Weight: 442.0 lbs.

BATTLE STRENGTH:
Scolipede charges at its enemies and jabs them over and over again with its horns. Once it's close enough, Scolipede will strike with its poisonous neck claws.

POWERFUL AGAINST: Dark, Grass, and Psychic

WEAK AGAINST: Fire, Flying, Psychic, and Rock

MEGAPEDE POKÉMON

SCOLIPEDE

STATS:

Type: Fire
Height: 4' 03"
Weight: 204.8 lbs.

BATTLE STRENGTH: One swing from Darmanitan's fiery fist can crush a dump truck like a soda can. Even when it's feeling weak, Darmanitan can battle on! It turns stiff like a stone statue and uses its mind to attack.

POWERFUL AGAINST: Bug, Grass, Ice, and Steel

WEAK AGAINST: Ground, Rock, and Water

BLAZING POKÉMON

DARMANITAN

STATS:

Type: Dark-Fighting
Height: 3' 07"
Weight: 66.1 lbs.

BATTLE STRENGTH: In battle, Scrafty is tougher than it looks — it spits toxic juice and can kick through concrete blocks. It's a good choice against Psychic-types, since Psychic-type moves do not affect it.

POWERFUL AGAINST: Dark, Ghost, Ice, Normal, Psychic, Rock, and Steel

WEAK AGAINST: Fighting and Flying

HOODLUM POKÉMON

SCRAFTY

STATS:

Type: Ghost
Height: 5' 07"
Weight: 168.7 lbs.

BATTLE STRENGTH: Don't get too close to Cofagrigus! It's said that anyone who tries to poach from this precious-looking Pokémon will get sucked into its coffin and come back out as a mummy.

POWERFUL AGAINST: Ghost and Psychic

WEAK AGAINST: Dark and Ghost

COFFIN POKÉMON

COFAGRIGUS

STATS:

Type: Rock-Flying
Height: 4' 07"
Weight: 70.5 lbs.

BATTLE STRENGTH: Fast as many cars, Archeops is known for outrunning its opponents. Moves like Rock Slide, Dragon Claw, and Acrobatics provide great offense, and it can use its Rock-type moves to counter Ice-type foes.

POWERFUL AGAINST: Bug, Fighting, Fire, Flying, Ice, and Grass

WEAK AGAINST: Electric, Ice, Rock, Steel, and Water

FIRST BIRD POKÉMON

ARCHEOPS

STATS:

Type: Dark
Height: 5' 03"
Weight: 178.8 lbs.

BATTLE STRENGTH: Zoroark uses trickery to protect the safety of its pack. It can use its amazing power to make landscapes appear and conceal its hideout from enemies. As a Dark-type, it is unaffected by Psychic-type attacks.

POWERFUL AGAINST: Ghost and Psychic

WEAK AGAINST: Bug and Fighting

ILLUSION FOX POKÉMON

ZOROARK

STATS:

Type: Psychic
Height: 3' 03"
Weight: 44.3 lbs.

BATTLE STRENGTH: Reuniclus and psychic power literally go hand in hand. When these Pokémon hold hands, their minds unite into one mighty force. Enemies, beware — those same arms are strong enough to crush stone!

POWERFUL AGAINST: Fighting and Poison

WEAK AGAINST: Bug, Dark, and Ghost

MULTIPLYING POKÉMON

REUNICLUS

STATS:

Type: Ice
Height: 4' 03"
Weight: 126.8 lbs.

BATTLE STRENGTH: During battle, Vanilluxe turns the water inside its body into ice that buries its foes in snow. It is weak against Rock-type Pokémon, but if it learns the move Mirror Shot, it can counter them.

POWERFUL AGAINST: Dragon, Flying, Grass, and Ground

WEAK AGAINST: Fighting, Fire, Rock, and Steel

SNOWSTORM POKÉMON

VANILLUXE

STATS:

Type: Bug-Steel
Height: 3' 03"
Weight: 72.8 lbs.

BATTLE STRENGTH: Brave Escavalier battles with two pointy spears. But its secret weapon is a Shelmet shell, which it uses to cover its body in full armor. It is unaffected by Poison-type attacks, but Fire-type attacks are especially strong against it.

POWERFUL AGAINST: Dark, Grass, Ice, Psychic, and Rock

WEAK AGAINST: Fire

CAVALRY POKÉMON

ESCAVALIER

Type: Water-Ghost
Height: 7' 03"
Weight: 297.6 lbs.

BATTLE STRENGTH: Jellicent may look harmless, but this Pokémon feeds on the life energy of its foes. Fighting- and Normal-type moves have no effect on it.

POWERFUL AGAINST: Fire, Ground, Psychic, and Rock

WEAK AGAINST: Dark, Electric, Ghost, and Grass

FLOATING POKÉMON

JELLICENT

STATS:

Type: Grass-Steel
Height: 3' 03"
Weight: 242.5 lbs.

BATTLE STRENGTH: When hanging from a cave ceiling, Ferrothorn pelts foes with steel spikes. If it runs into a foe on the ground, it uses its three arms to pack a triple punch. Ferrothorn shrugs off Poison-type attacks, but Fire-type attacks are very effective against it.

POWERFUL AGAINST: Ground, Ice, Rock, and Water

WEAK AGAINST: Fire and Fighting

THORN POD POKÉMON

FERROTHORN

STATS:

Type: Electric
Height: 6' 11"
Weight: 177.5 lbs.

BATTLE STRENGTH: Eelektross's mouth acts like a vacuum that sucks in enemies. Then it sinks in its sharp teeth and delivers an electric shock. Eelektross has the Ability Levitate, which allows it to withstand Ground-type attacks.

POWERFUL AGAINST: Flying and Water

WEAK AGAINST: Ground

ELEFISH POKÉMON

EELEKTROSS

Type: Ghost-Fire
Height: 3' 03"
Weight: 75.6 lbs.

BATTLE STRENGTH:
Chandelure makes its flames dance to put its opponents in a trance. Some Chandelure have the Ability Flash Fire, which means Fire-type attacks against them just make their own Fire-type moves more powerful. Spooky!

POWERFUL AGAINST: Bug, Ghost, Grass, Ice, Psychic, and Steel

WEAK AGAINST: Dark, Ghost, Ground, Rock, and Water

LURING POKÉMON

CHANDELURE

STATS:

Type: Ice
Height: 8' 06"
Weight: 573.2 lbs.

BATTLE STRENGTH: With one simple breath, Beartic can turn the air around it into icicles that it transforms into sharp teeth or talons — a great tool for fighting foes.

POWERFUL AGAINST: Dragon, Flying, Grass, and Ground

WEAK AGAINST: Fighting, Fire, Rock, and Steel

FREEZING POKÉMON

BEARTIC

STATS:

Type: Bug
Height: 2' 07"
Weight: 55.8 lbs.

BATTLE STRENGTH: Beware of Accelgor's lightning-fast battle moves! It can use ninja-like attacks in combat. To defend itself from dehydration, it keeps its body wrapped in thin layers of skin.

POWERFUL AGAINST: Dark, Grass, and Psychic

WEAK AGAINST: Fire, Flying, and Rock

SHELL OUT POKÉMON

ACCELGOR

STATS:

Type: Fighting
Height: 4' 07"
Weight: 78.3 lbs.

BATTLE STRENGTH: Mienshao can move its arms so fast, foes don't even see its blows coming. As it swings, the long hair on its arms acts like a whip. *Ouch!* Mienshao is weak against Psychic-type attacks, but it can learn U-turn, which can help it defend itself against Psychic-type Pokémon.

POWERFUL AGAINST: Dark, Ice, Normal, Rock, and Steel

WEAK AGAINST: Flying and Psychic

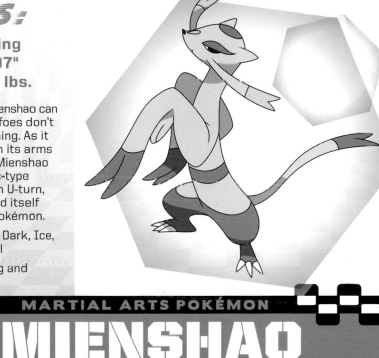

MARTIAL ARTS POKÉMON

MIENSHAO

STATS:

Type: Ground-Ghost
Height: 9' 02"
Weight: 727.5 lbs.

BATTLE STRENGTH: This Pokémon can fly through the sky at the speed of sound. Its type combination makes it resistant to Normal-, Fighting-, and Electric-type attacks.

POWERFUL AGAINST: Electric, Fire, Ghost, Poison, Psychic, Rock, and Steel

WEAK AGAINST: Dark, Ghost, Grass, Ice, and Water

AUTOMATON POKÉMON

GOLURK

STATS:

Type: Normal
Height: 5' 03"
Weight: 208.6 lbs.

BATTLE STRENGTH: Bouffalant loves to headbutt, and can do it with enough force to stop a train dead in its tracks. But Bouffalant doesn't feel a thing — its fur cushions the blow.

POWERFUL AGAINST: Normal-types are not strong against any particular type, but Ghost-type attacks cannot damage them.

WEAK AGAINST: Fighting

BOUFFALANT

STATS:

Type: Dark-Flying
Height: 3' 11"
Weight: 87.1 lbs.

BATTLE STRENGTH:
Mandibuzz can spot prey while flying high, and it swoops down in a flash. It uses the bones of its foes to make its home. So keep your eye on the sky lest your Pokémon become part of its collection!

POWERFUL AGAINST: Bug, Fighting, Ghost, Grass, and Psychic

WEAK AGAINST: Electric, Ice, and Rock

BONE VULTURE POKÉMON

MANDIBUZZ

STATS:

Type: Bug-Steel
Height: 1' 00"
Weight: 72.8 lbs.

BATTLE STRENGTH: When Durant come face-to-face with their foe, Heatmor, they attack as one. It is especially weak against Fire-type attacks — unless it learns the Ground-type attack Dig to counter Fire-type foes. Poison-type attacks don't affect Durant.

POWERFUL AGAINST: Dark, Grass, Ice, Psychic, and Rock

WEAK AGAINST: Fire

IRON ANT POKÉMON

DURANT

STATS:

Type: Bug-Fire
Height: 5' 03"
Weight: 101.4 lbs.

BATTLE STRENGTH: During a heated battle, Volcarona's six wings shed scales of hot ashes. These embers surround the battle in a ring of flames. Its Flame Body Ability can burn opponents who attack it directly, but it is especially vulnerable to Rock-type attacks.

POWERFUL AGAINST: Bug, Dark, Grass, Ice, Psychic, and Steel

WEAK AGAINST: Flying, Rock, and Water

SUN POKÉMON

VOLCARONA

SERPERIOR

REGAL POKÉMON

STATS:

Type: Grass
Height: 10' 10"
Weight: 138.9 lbs.

BATTLE STRENGTH: Serperior really uses its head in battle. It scares foes by lifting its head and glaring. One look can stop an opponent in its tracks. Its Ability, Overgrow, powers up its Grass-type moves when it's low on energy.

POWERFUL AGAINST: Ground, Rock, and Water

WEAK AGAINST: Bug, Fire, Flying, Ice, and Poison

SAMUROTT

FORMIDABLE POKÉMON

STATS:

Type: Water
Height: 4' 11"
Weight: 208.6 lbs.

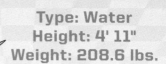

BATTLE STRENGTH: Samurott's cry frightens foes, and its battle stare silences them. But its most powerful weapon is the sword it can draw from the armor on its front legs. It can learn the Bug-type moves Megahorn and Fury Cutter to use against Grass-type foes.

POWERFUL AGAINST: Fire, Ground, and Rock

WEAK AGAINST: Electric and Grass

STATS:

Type: Normal
Height: 3' 11"
Weight: 134.5 lbs.

BATTLE STRENGTH: Stoutland can learn the move Odor Sleuth, which makes its Normal-type moves affect Ghost-types. It can also learn the moves Ice Fang, Fire Fang, and Thunder Fang to lend some bite to its bark!

POWERFUL AGAINST: Normal-types are not strong against any particular type, but Ghost-type attacks cannot damage them.

WEAK AGAINST: Fighting

SIMISAGE
THORN MONKEY POKÉMON

STATS:

Type: Grass
Height: 3' 07"
Weight: 67.2 lbs.

BATTLE STRENGTH: Simisage is a real wild child. Look out for its spiky tail in battle — this Grass-type likes to swing it around its opponents. It can also learn the powerful move Seed Bomb.

POWERFUL AGAINST: Ground, Rock, and Water

WEAK AGAINST: Bug, Fire, Flying, Ice, and Poison

SIMIPOUR

GEYSER POKÉMON

STATS:

Type: Water
Height: 3' 03"
Weight: 63.9 lbs.

BATTLE STRENGTH: Simipour soaks up water through its tail and stores it in the tufts on its head. Keep an eye on that tail — Simipour can use it as a powerful hose, spraying water blasts strong enough to break through a concrete wall!

POWERFUL AGAINST: Fire, Ground, and Rock

WEAK AGAINST: Electric and Grass

ZEBSTRIKA

THUNDERBOLT POKÉMON

STATS:

Type: Electric
Height: 5' 03"
Weight: 175.3 lbs.

BATTLE STRENGTH: Zebstrika is fast as lightning, and its gallop booms like thunder. Whatever you do, don't make it mad — its long white mane can zap you with supercharged lightning bolts! Opponents' Electric-type moves can actually make some Zebstrika even faster.

POWERFUL AGAINST: Flying and Water

WEAK AGAINST: Ground

SWOOBAT

COURTING POKÉMON

STATS:

Type: Psychic-Flying
Height: 2' 11"
Weight: 23.1 lbs.

BATTLE STRENGTH: If a male Swoobat wants to battle, it emits a sound wave tough enough to turn rocks to dust. It can learn the Heart Stamp move, which makes its opponents flinch.

POWERFUL AGAINST: Dug, Fighting, Grass, and Poison

WEAK AGAINST: Dark, Electric, Ghost, Ice, and Rock

CONKELDURR

STATS:

Type: Fighting
Height: 4' 07"
Weight: 191.8 lbs.

BATTLE STRENGTH: Don't be fooled by Conkeldurr's two concrete canes. It might use them for walking, but it can also swing them around — which sure comes in handy during battle!

POWERFUL AGAINST: Dark, Ice, Normal, Rock, and Steel

WEAK AGAINST: Flying and Psychic

THROH

JUDO POKÉMON

STATS:

Type: Fighting
Height: 4' 03"
Weight: 122.4 lbs.

BATTLE STRENGTH: If you see Throh tightening its vine belt, look out! That's how it increases its power. Tall foes should beware: Throh never misses the chance to lift a larger opponent.

POWERFUL AGAINST: Dark, Ice, Normal, Rock, and Steel

WEAK AGAINST: Flying and Psychic

LEAVANNY

NURTURING POKÉMON

STATS:

Type: Bug-Grass
Height: 3' 11"
Weight: 45.2 lbs.

BATTLE STRENGTH: During battle, Leavanny slashes at opponents with the leaf blades on its arms. Whatever you do, don't get caught in the super-sticky silk it shoots. Its String Shot move is famous for tangling up foes and slowing them down.

POWERFUL AGAINST: Dark, Grass, Ground, Psychic, Rock, and Water

WEAK AGAINST: Bug, Fire, Flying, Ice, Poison, and Rock

KROOKODILE

INTIMIDATION POKÉMON

STATS:

Type: Ground-Dark
Height: 4' 11"
Weight: 212.3 lbs.

BATTLE STRENGTH: Krookodile's chompers can crush a car, and its eyes are just as sharp! It has built-in binoculars that can spot foes far in the distance. Krookodile's type combo allows it to shrug off Electric- and Psychic-type attacks.

POWERFUL AGAINST: Electric, Fire, Ghost, Poison, Psychic, Rock, and Steel

WEAK AGAINST: Bug, Fighting, Grass, Ice, and Water

CRUSTLE

STONE HOME POKÉMON

STATS:

Type: Bug-Rock
Height: 4' 07"
Weight: 440.9 lbs.

BATTLE STRENGTH: If an enemy challenges its turf, Crustle will go head-to-head in battle — er, make that boulder-to-boulder. It's not known for its speed, but it can use the Shell Smash move to sacrifice some of its armor and boost its offense.

POWERFUL AGAINST: Bug, Dark, Fire, Flying, Grass, Ice, and Psychic

WEAK AGAINST: Rock, Steel, and Water

SIGILYPH

AVIANOID POKÉMON

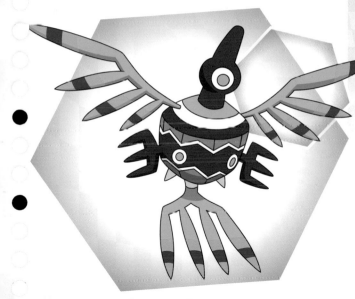

STATS:

Type: Psychic-Flying
Height: 4' 07"
Weight: 30.9 lbs.

BATTLE STRENGTH: If an enemy invades the ancient city they protect, Sigilyph will use their psychic power to destroy them. It is at a disadvantage against Dark-types like Zoroark, but it can learn lots of powerful Flying-type moves, like Air Slash.

POWERFUL AGAINST: Bug, Fighting, Grass, and Poison

WEAK AGAINST: Dark, Electric, Ghost, Ice, and Rock

CARRACOSTA

PROTOTURTLE POKÉMON

STATS:

Type: Water-Rock
Height: 3' 11"
Weight: 178.6 lbs.

BATTLE STRENGTH: Choose your battlefield carefully, because Carracosta can battle on land or in the ocean! Its chompers can gnaw through steel and rocks. It is especially weak against Grass-type attacks. For a good battle match-up, try Carracosta vs. Crustle or Archeops.

POWERFUL AGAINST: Bug, Fire, Flying, Ground, Ice, and Rock

WEAK AGAINST: Electric, Fighting, Grass, and Ground

GARBODOR

TRASH HEAP POKÉMON

STATS:

Type: Poison
Height: 6' 03"
Weight: 236.6 lbs.

BATTLE STRENGTH: Garbodor's right hand has three fingers that spray a toxic liquid. Enemies should keep a safe distance — Garbodor likes to burp in the faces of its foes, and the smelly poison gas it belches can finish them off. Excadrill would be a tough opponent.

POWERFUL AGAINST: Grass

WEAK AGAINST: Ground and Psychic

GOTHITELLE

ASTRAL BODY POKÉMON

STATS:

Type: Psychic
Height: 4' 11"
Weight: 97.0 lbs.

BATTLE STRENGTH: Gothitelle can trick foes with moves like Fake Tears, Tickle, and Charm. Its Psychic and Future Sight moves are particularly strong. But Gothitelle Trainers should beware Dark-type Pokémon.

POWERFUL AGAINST: Fighting and Poison

WEAK AGAINST: Bug, Dark, and Ghost

SWANNA

WHITE BIRD POKÉMON

STATS:

Type: Water-Flying
Height: 4' 03"
Weight: 53.4 lbs.

BATTLE STRENGTH: Look out for Swanna's long neck and pointed beak! They help Swanna peck fiercely at its foes. Electric-type moves are especially damaging to this Pokémon, but it can learn powerful Flying-type moves like Brave Bird and Hurricane.

POWERFUL AGAINST: Bug, Fighting, Fire, Ground, Grass, and Rock

WEAK AGAINST: Electric and Rock

EMOLGA

SKY SQUIRREL POKÉMON

Type: Electric-Flying
Height: 1' 04"
Weight: 11.0 lbs.

BATTLE STRENGTH: Emolga's cheeks might seem chubby and adorable, but they are filled with electric power. As it soars through the air, Emolga uses its yellow cape to zap its opponents with the electricity it's stored.

POWERFUL AGAINST: Bug, Fighting, Flying, Grass, and Water

WEAK AGAINST: Ice and Rock

AMOONGUSS

MUSHROOM POKÉMON

STATS:

Type: Grass-Poison
Height: 2' 00"
Weight: 23.1 lbs.

BATTLE STRENGTH:
Amoonguss's secret weapon is its dance. It hopes its smooth moves and Poké Ball markings will lure prey its way. It can also learn the move Spore to put foes to sleep, or Toxic to poison them.

POWERFUL AGAINST: Water, Grass, Ground, and Rock

WEAK AGAINST: Fire, Ice, Flying, and Psychic

GALVANTULA

ELESPIDER POKÉMON

STATS:

Type: Bug-Electric
Height: 2' 07"
Weight: 31.5 lbs.

BATTLE STRENGTH: Galvantula spins electrified thread that shocks the prey trapped in its web. When it is under attack, it uses the same thread to create a protective wall around itself.

POWERFUL AGAINST: Dark, Flying, Grass, Psychic, and Water

WEAK AGAINST: Fire and Rock

KLINKLANG

GEAR POKÉMON

STATS:

Type: Steel
Height: 2' 00"
Weight: 178.6 lbs.

BATTLE STRENGTH: To power up, the gear with the red center spins around superfast. When its core is all charged up, Klinklang fires energy attacks from its ring of spikes. It can learn powerful moves like Hyper Beam and Zap Cannon.

POWERFUL AGAINST: Ice and Rock

WEAK AGAINST: Fighting, Fire, and Ground

BEHEEYEM

CEREBRAL POKÉMON

STATS:

Type: Psychic
Height: 3' 03"
Weight: 76.1 lbs.

BATTLE STRENGTH: Beheeyem can mess with your memory in a flash! It uses its psychic power to control its opponents' brains. It can learn the move Confusion to befuddle its foes.

POWERFUL AGAINST: Fighting and Poison

WEAK AGAINST: Bug, Dark, and Ghost

HAXORUS

AXE JAW POKÉMON

STATS:

Type: Dragon
Height: 5' 11"
Weight: 232.6 lbs.

BATTLE STRENGTH: Haxorus is covered in tough armor on the outside. When it needs to protect its turf, it lashes out with fangs sharp enough to slice through steel.

POWERFUL AGAINST: Dragon

WEAK AGAINST: Dragon and Ice

CRYGONAL

CRYSTALLIZING POKÉMON

STATS:

Type: Ice
Height: 3' 07"
Weight: 326.3 lbs.

BATTLE STRENGTH: Crygonal ties its foes up in chains made of ice crystal. When things heat up, it disappears into thin air by turning into steam, since its body is made of water. It uses its Ability, Levitate, to withstand Ground-type attacks.

POWERFUL AGAINST: Dragon, Flying, Grass, and Ground

WEAK AGAINST: Fighting, Fire, Rock, and Steel

STUNFISK

STATS:

Type: Ground-Electric
Height: 2' 04"
Weight: 24.3 lbs.

BATTLE STRENGTH: Stunfisk has a stiff skin, and it likes to bury its body in the sand. When foes try to walk all over it, Stunfisk just smiles and shocks them with electricity!

POWERFUL AGAINST: Fire, Flying, Electric, Poison, Rock, Steel, and Water

WEAK AGAINST: Grass, Ground, Ice, and Water

DRUDDIGON

STATS:

Type: Dragon
Height: 5' 03"
Weight: 306.4 lbs.

BATTLE STRENGTH: The Cave Pokémon is truly hardheaded. Its noggin is like a rock — a great shield in battle. It uses its sharp claws to catch its prey. It can learn the Fighting-type move Superpower, which is effective against Ice-type Pokémon.

POWERFUL AGAINST: Dragon

WEAK AGAINST: Ice and Dragon

BISHARP

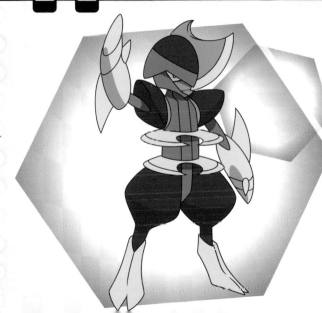

STATS:

Type: Dark-Steel
Height: 5' 03"
Weight: 154.3 lbs.

BATTLE STRENGTH: Bisharp can learn a wide range of Normal-, Dark-, and Steel-type moves. It is especially weak against Fighting-type attacks, but Poison- and Psychic-type attacks have no effect on it.

POWERFUL AGAINST: Ghost, Ice, Rock, and Psychic

WEAK AGAINST: Fighting, Fire, and Ground

BRAVIARY

VALIANT POKÉMON

Type: Normal-Flying
Height: 4' 11"
Weight: 90.4 lbs.

BATTLE STRENGTH: Braviary is strong enough to carry a car, but its real strength is its fearlessness. It will defend a friend no matter the danger, and it considers battle wounds badges of honor.

POWERFUL AGAINST: Grass, Fighting, and Bug

WEAK AGAINST: Electric, Ice, and Rock

HEATMOR

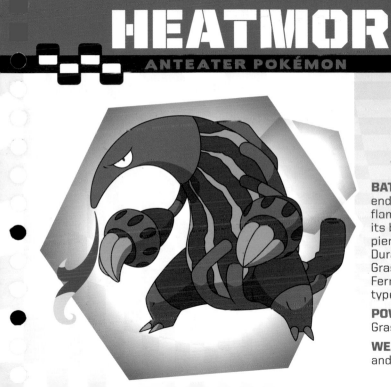

STATS:

Type: Fire
Height: 4' 07"
Weight: 127.9 lbs.

BATTLE STRENGTH: At the end of Heatmor's long nose is a flame tongue lit by the blaze in its belly. With fiery licks, it can pierce the steel skin of its prey, Durant. It is also tough versus Grass- and Steel-types like Ferrothorn, and Bug- and Grass-types like Leavanny.

POWERFUL AGAINST: Bug, Grass, Ice, and Steel

WEAK AGAINST: Ground, Rock, and Water

HYDREIGON

BRUTAL POKÉMON

STATS:

Type: Dark-Dragon
Height: 5' 11"
Weight: 352.7 lbs.

BATTLE STRENGTH: Three heads are better than one! Hydreigon only has one brain, but the noggins on its arms add strength to its attacks. Its Levitate Ability makes it immune to Ground-type attacks.

POWERFUL AGAINST: Dragon, Ghost, and Psychic

WEAK AGAINST: Bug, Dragon, Fighting, and Ice